The Monumental Disco

The Monumental Discovery

Mark Oestreicher

Tyndale House Publishers, Inc.
Wheaton, Illinois

Books in the Choice Adventures series

1 *The Mysterious Old Church*

2 *The Smithsonian Connection*

3 *The Underground Railroad*

4 *The Rain Forest Mystery*

5 *The Quarterback Sneak*

6 *The Monumental Discovery*

7 *The Abandoned Gold Mine*

8 *The Hazardous Homestead*

Library of Congress Cataloging-in-Publication Data

Oestreicher, Mark
    The monumental discovery / Mark Oestreicher
        p.   cm. — (Choice adventures ; #6)
    Summary: The reader's choices control the adventures of a group of
friends who make a trip to Washington, D.C., to try out a new camera.
    ISBN 0-8423-5030-6
    1. Plot-your-own stories.   [1. Plot-your-own stories.
2. Adventure and adventurers—Fiction.   3. Washington (D.C.)—Fiction.
4. Christian life—Fiction.]   I. Title.   II. Series.
PZ7.O292Mo   1992
[Fic]—dc20   91-38123

Printed in the United States of America

99   98   97   96   95   94   93   92
 9   8   7   6   5   4   3   2   1

"**N**o way!" shouted Willy.

"I know, I could hardly believe it when I opened it either."

Willy stared with envy at Sam's new possession—an expensive 35mm camera.

"And that's not even the best part," Sam bragged to his best friend. "Look at this!"

He reached into the nylon carrying case and pulled out a big black cylinder.

"What's that?" questioned Willy.

"It's a telephoto lens. And not just any telephoto lens. It's a *500mm* mirrored telephoto lens."

This meant nothing to Willy. In fact, it barely meant anything to Sam. But he knew it was cool. His uncle Jeff was a professional photographer, and he had given the camera to Sam that morning for his birthday, even though his birthday wasn't really until next week. They didn't usually give such fancy gifts in his family, but his uncle got a great deal on some used equipment.

"Do you remember my uncle Jeff?" asked Sam. Jeff had been in town for a week the last summer and spent a lot of time with the boys. They'd had a blast together.

"Yeah, did he give this to you? Oh, man, . . . I'm so jealous," Willy admitted.

After twisting and turning the camera for a while, the

2

two boys finally got the regular lens off. Then they put the telephoto lens on the camera. Sam hadn't had a chance to put the special lens on since he had received it in the mail. Taking off the lens cap, he put the back of the camera to his face, looked through the viewfinder, and gasped.

"This is incredible!" Sam shouted. "You can see forever!"

The boys were sitting on a bench outside the Freeze, their favorite hangout. Across the street was the Common, a park in the center of town.

From where Sam was sitting he could clearly see all the details on the front of the old church across the Common. In fact, it seemed too close through the lens. If he focused correctly, he could even see inside the building.

"There's Mr. Whitehead."

"Where?" asked Willy.

"Inside the church. He's looking at some papers."

In his excitement, Willy grabbed for the camera. "You can see that far? That's so cool!"

Sam was startled by Willy's lunge for the camera and pulled away quickly. "What do you think you're doing?" he snapped. "Do you have any idea how much this baby cost?"

"Well, I just wanted to have a look too," muttered Willy.

"Never, never grab for my camera like that!" Sam was behaving very different from his normal funny manner.

"OK, I won't. You don't have to be such a jerk about it." Willy waited a few impatient moments, then said, "Can I look?"

CHOICE ➤

If Sam lets Willy look through the camera, turn to page 39.

If Sam's still a bit cautious about letting others use his camera, turn to page 55.

4

By the time Jim got his turn with the camera, the boys had been up in the monument for forty-five minutes. Those who had used the camera first were getting pretty bored and were just about ready to leave.

"I won't take very long, guys," Jim said, sensing their impatience. He fumbled with the lens, trying to get it focused. "It's hard to tell what you're focusing on when you can't see the whole picture."

Finally Jim got the camera focused.

"Whoa! Guys! I just saw an accident!"

"What do you mean?" Boredom ceased, and everyone surrounded Jim, waiting to hear what he was seeing.

"Oh, man! The guy's leaving! I can't believe it!" Jim was getting loud, and other people in the viewing room were listening to the story.

"Jim," Pete began with a calming voice, "stay focused on the car. Follow him. But tell us what happened."

Jim blurted the whole thing out in one long strung-together sentence: "When I finally got the camera focused, I focused it on a car that was driving down an alley, and there was this old lady bending over a garbage can, and she stood up as the car came toward her, and I don't know if the guy didn't see her or what, but he just nailed her! Just nailed her!"

Jim followed Pete's instructions and never took his

eyes off the car; it was now going along Fifteenth Street, near the base of the monument.

"Anyhow," Jim continued as he followed the car with the camera, "the lady flew up onto his hood, and he stopped real fast, throwing her back onto the pavement. The guy jumped out of the car and ran over to her. Then he just walked back to his car."

"Wow!" Willy gasped. "Is that all?"

"No, he was looking back over his shoulder at her on the way back to the car, and he fell right over the trash can she was looking in, right on his face—looked like he hurt his cheek pretty bad."

"Well, he must have gone to get some help," guessed Willy. "I mean, there's no reason to suspect he just hit her and left, right?"

"Now there is," answered Jim.

Chris was frustrated with the lack of information and not being able to see anything himself. "What are you talking about, Jim? And this better not be a joke!"

For the first time since the incident began, Jim looked away from the window. He lowered the camera and looked straight at Chris. "I would never joke about something like this."

"OK, OK, just tell us why there's reason to suspect him."

"Oh yeah. Because he didn't go to get help. He parked his car outside that big building and went inside."

"What building?" asked Pete.

Jim looked through the camera again, then up at the reference map above the window.

6

"Here," he said, pointing. "It's this one behind the Air and Space Museum."

The Ringers knew that museum well because of an earlier adventure they'd had there.

Pete looked up the number of the building Jim had pointed at. "Department of Health and Human Services," he announced.

Chris took over the conversation. "First things first. We need to call someone about that lady in the alley."

"I'll take care of that if you'll tell me where she is." The voice came from one of the people standing behind the boys. Everyone turned around to see a security guard. "We've got an emergency phone right over here—just tell me where she is."

Jim found her with the camera and showed the guard the location.

After the guard left to make the phone call and the other onlookers had wandered away, Chris gathered the group around him and spoke in a low voice. "Ringers, this calls for action. We know where the man is. Maybe he's guilty, maybe he's innocent. And who knows if that lady's OK. The way I see it, we've got two choices. One, we go to the alley to see how she's doing and check if the man called for help too. Or, two, we go to the Health building and look for the guy."

"What would we do if we found him?" asked Sam, a bit shook up by the whole thing.

"I don't know. We'll figure that out if we find him."

CHOICE ➤

If the boys go the alley, turn to page 117.

If they go to the government building, turn to page 26.

8

As soon as the door to the rest room closed, Pete mumbled, "What a hypocritical jerk!"

"Pete," Willy said with frustration in his voice, "why do you always use words I don't know?"

Chris answered for Pete. "Maybe it's because you have the vocabulary of a wood tick."

Willy refused to submit to Chris's teasing this time. "OK, Chris, maybe you're right. So how 'bout if *you* explain what Pete said."

"Yeah!" chimed all the rest of the guys.

"Fine . . . uh . . . what did you say again, Pete?"

Willy and Sam were already laughing. They didn't care if Chris had a good answer or not.

"I said Senator Dunlap was a hypocritical jerk."

"Oh yeah, that's what I thought you said."

Now it was Willy's turn to tease. He said in a singsong voice, "Oh yeah, that's what I thought you said—I just don't have a clue what it means!"

"I do too know what it means!" Chris was getting defensive. "It means that the senator is two-faced. He says one thing but does another."

Pete finished for him. "Yeah, a lot of Christians are that way. They say they stand for Christ, but they don't live it at all. In fact, I remember our Sunday school teacher, Miss Whitehead—"

"My grandpa's sister," Jim reminded Pete.

"Oh yeah, I keep forgetting that. Anyway, she once showed us this verse in the Bible that says something like 'I wish you were either hot or cold, but because you're lukewarm, I spit you out of my mouth.'"

"Gross."

"Cool."

"Miss Whitehead said it means that God would rather people really live for him or not live for him at all than claim to live for him and give people a poor idea of what that means."

"Can you imagine getting spit out of God's mouth?" Sam was having a hard time getting past the illustration.

"What's the point?" Chris was getting impatient.

"Senator Rod Dunlap, defender of humanity," Pete started, as if he were introducing the senator, "is the same guy we saw hit that bag lady in the alley—maybe even killed her. Then he drives away from it like nothing happened. He knows it would be major slime on his record to have hit *anybody*, let alone a homeless person, so he's protecting himself at her expense."

"Wow, he *is* a hypocritical jerk," said Willy, totally serious.

Chris drew the conclusions. "If hitting her might have hurt his career, then our film can waste his face. We got proof that he did it and then ran and didn't report it. If people found out, it would completely end his career, right?"

"Definitely," confirmed Pete.

"You couldn't be more right."

10

The boys froze. They thought they were alone in the rest room. But that last comment had come from one of the bathroom stalls. Someone had been in there listening to them the whole time!

A very large man stepped out of the stall. "Hello, boys. I'm Senator Dunlap's personal aid. You can call me Mr. Rey." He was using a friendly tone of voice, the kind of "friendly tone" adults fake when they're holding back from completely pulverizing someone. The guys began to sweat again.

"Well, nice to meet you, Mr. Rey. We'll be on our way now," Chris said involuntarily as he moved toward the door. None of the other guys had moved a single muscle. They were all staring at Mr. Rey with their mouths hanging open.

"I don't think you'll be leaving just yet," Mr. Rey shot at Chris.

Chris stopped in his tracks.

Mr. Rey continued, "We got a real problem here, boys. You see, if what you say is true, then not only will *he* be out of a job . . ." He paused and stooped over, sticking his face right in Willy's. Then he finished his sentence with a snarl: *"I'll* be out of a job. You don't want that to happen, do you?"

"No sir," Willy whimpered. He felt like he might cry. He couldn't remember when he had ever been so scared.

"So, I'll tell you what we'll do." Mr. Rey straightened to his full height again and addressed the whole gang. "You boys hand over that film and promise to keep your mouths closed, and we'll forget this whole thing ever happened. Otherwise, there just might be some pretty severe consequences."

CHOICE

If the guys hand over the film, turn to page 105.

If they run, turn to page 17.

If they try to talk their way out of this, turn to page 76.

12

"**I** don't even see the question here." Pete was answering his own question. And he was, once again, in his data-processing mode. "I mean, we can't officially do anything about it ourselves—we're just kids."

Pete wasn't even looking at anyone. He stared straight ahead and continued processing.

"But we do have an obligation to help the guy if he's hurt. The obvious choice is to tell that policeman over there what we've seen."

"No way!" Sam didn't like the idea. "What if he decides to take my camera away as evidence?"

Chris laughed. "Don't be a geek. He's not gonna take your camera."

"Well," said Sam, realizing he was being a bit overcautious, "I guess that's a good plan then."

The policeman could tell they were talking about him, and by the time Sam agreed to Pete's idea, the officer was right next to them on his horse.

"Can I help you boys?" His voice came from somewhere over their heads.

"Aaah!" Sam, Chris, and Willy all yelled in surprise. They hadn't seen the officer ride over to them.

"You scared us half to death!" Chris was puffing like he had just run a marathon.

The officer had a big smile on his face, showing that

he had obviously gotten a big kick out of surprising the boys.

Pete jumped in and told their story to the officer.

When Pete finished, the policeman said, "You boys did the right thing in telling me. Now can you tell me one more thing?" He looked right at Sam. "Is the man still there?"

Sam immediately resumed his photography stance and peered across the Mall. "Yup!"

"OK, I'll radio for another officer to check it out. You boys wait here for a minute." He led his horse a few feet away and started talking into his walkie-talkie.

After a minute Chris walked over to the officer.

"Where's he think he's going?" asked Sam. None of the guys could hear Chris or the officer, but they talked for a minute or so.

The horse clopped back over to the gang, and the officer explained, "The situation is being checked out right now. But in the meantime I will have to take your camera as evidence." He looked right at Sam and held out his hand.

Sam gasped. "My camera? You need my camera as evidence? I can't believe this!" He turned to Chris. "You even called me a geek for thinking he might want it. Who's the geek now?"

"You are," Chris said with a big smile on his face.

"What?" Sam froze in his tracks. He was totally confused.

"You're the geek 'cause you fell for it!" Chris started laughing hard.

After the other guys figured out that Chris had set up the joke with the officer, they all joined in the laughter. It

14

was a clean, slam-dunk practical joke, and Sam had fallen for it all the way.

Within seconds, the officer and even Sam were laughing.

CHOICE

Turn to page 35.

"**W**e gotta go see if he's OK," said Chris. He started toward the Mall, not even waiting for the others.

Everyone followed, even though a couple of the guys weren't sure this was the best plan. Soon they were all running full tilt.

It took much longer than they expected, since everything had seemed so close through the telephoto lens.

"Whew!" Sam was whipped. "Whose brilliant idea was it to run?"

As they walked up to the man, they saw that he was now on his hands and knees crawling around.

"Hey, mister," Chris called out. "We saw you get kicked—or, I mean, he saw you get kicked." Chris pointed at Sam. "And we wondered if you were OK."

The boys were all standing over the man. He was scary looking, and everyone but Chris backed up a step after they got a look at his face. He had dark, beady, bloodshot eyes and long, stringy hair.

The man scowled at them—he didn't answer.

"Hey, look what I found. What do you think this is?" Jim was walking up from behind the boys with something in his hand.

The scene that followed happened so fast that it was almost a blur.

Everyone wheeled around. The Ringers and the

scowling man all focused on the little plastic bag in Jim's hand. The guys froze. The man gasped.

Chris whispered to no one in particular, "Drugs!" None of them had actually seen any drugs before, but the bag looked just like they all expected.

The man lunged at Jim. "That's mine!" he snapped, in a very intense voice. "Give it to me *now!*"

CHOICE ⇒

If Jim gives the drugs to the man, turn to page 62.

If Jim tries to keep the man from getting them, turn to page 42.

In his fear, Willy forgot they were in a small closed room with no quick escape routes. He yelled, "Run!" turned around, and planted his face in the rest room door.

Somehow he managed to get the door open and blazed into the hallway.

In that instant of complete confusion, the gang would have followed any suggestion. Everyone bolted after Willy.

"Where do you think you're going?" Mr. Rey yelled as he grabbed Sam's arm. There were just too many guys to escape quickly through the narrow door. Sam, the one with the film, had been caught. The rest of the guys cleared the rest room.

"You know," Mr. Rey began, anger rising in his voice, "that was really stupid. What do you think I'm going to have to do with you now?" Sam struggled to get away.

He was terrified—not just because of Mr. Rey's threat, but because Mr. Rey was so angry. Sam knew that people can do violent things when they're mad.

"Give me that!" Mr. Rey ripped the camera from Sam's hands. The strap around Sam's neck choked him as the huge man yanked it.

What happened next would go down in Sam's memory as a miracle.

The door to the rest room swung open, and a man in

a custodian's outfit rolled in a cleaning cart. He took on a startled expression as his eyes took in the scene.

"Dad! Save me!" Sam yelled.

"Dad?" Mr. Rey echoed, still clutching the camera.

"Sam, what's going on here?" asked Mr. Ramirez. Sam's mom and dad both worked for a company that had contracts to clean many of the big public buildings. Sam had no idea his dad would be in the Health building that day.

Mr. Rey, a bit flustered, tried his best to think fast. "Uh, your son has a nice camera here." Then he turned his attention to Sam and in a fake friendly voice said, "Thanks for letting me look at it."

With that, Mr. Rey handed the camera over to Sam and quickly left the rest room. Mr. Ramirez wanted to stop him but thought better of it.

Sam was so glad to see his dad he was almost crying.

The other guys came back into the rest room after seeing Mr. Rey leave so quickly. Together, they spilled the whole story to Sam's dad.

Mr. Ramirez took the afternoon off work in order to escort the shaken gang to the FBI building, where Pete's dad worked.

And before the day ended, "the wheels of justice were turning," as Pete put it.

They told their story to Chris's mom as they rode home on the train. She shook her head when Sam finished with his version of the final moments of the rest room rescue. She was speaking to Chris as she concluded, "Sometimes I think you hang out with the Hardy Boys."

They all just smiled.

THE END
Turn to page 120.

20

Willy remembered something his old Sunday school teacher, Miss Whitehead, said once: "Sometimes it takes more courage to say no than to say yes." It hadn't made much sense at the time, but it sure did now. Still, he couldn't muster the courage to say no before this went any farther.

Before they knew it, all six boys were up in Randy's attic. It was cluttered with boxes and dusty suitcases.

"C'mon. Over here." Randy was already at the end of the attic motioning for the other boys to follow him.

A small hexagon-shaped window let bright streams of sunlight into the hot, dusty room.

"Hurry up and give me that camera. Ronda should be coming into her room any time now." Randy was rushing them and seemed a little bit nervous.

Sam was dying. He couldn't believe he was doing this, especially with his brand new camera. His uncle Jeff would never have given it to him had he known how it would be used. Sam couldn't even look at Willy. He knew this was wrong but didn't know if he could handle whatever look Willy might shoot his way.

Reluctantly, Sam handed his camera to Chip. Chip seemed like the calmest person there and the least likely to hurt the new equipment.

Chip moved toward the window and lifted the camera to his eye.

The lens on the front of the camera was longer than any Chip was used to. Before he knew it, he had put it right through the window.

In the quiet of the moment the shattering glass sounded louder than it really was.

"Oh no! You idiot!" Randy was freaking out. "I can't believe you did that! My parents are going to kill me!"

Sam interrupted, "Who cares about the stupid window, my camera better be OK!" He was starting to freak out too.

CHOICE ➤

If the buys all agree to stop before they get into more trouble, turn to page 96.

If they calm down and continue their plan, turn to page 100.

22

The boys stared at each other in disbelief.

Willy vocalized their collective thoughts. "Can you believe it?"

Pete quickly put his pointer finger to his lips, signaling that no one should talk. He then pointed to one of the bathroom stalls. The door was closed, and it was obviously occupied. Pete mouthed silently, "It would be better to talk in complete privacy," then motioned toward the door. A public rest room wasn't the most private place in the world.

The rest of the gang nodded.

Without saying one word, they left the rest room and walked on until they were outside the building. Just to be cautious, they continued in silence for another block and a half.

Finally Willy couldn't stand it any longer. "Can you believe it?" he blurted.

All the guys burst into nervous laughter.

"He asked us to take his picture!"

"We didn't even have to look for him!"

"But he *thought* we were looking for him!"

Comments of amazement continued for two or three minutes. Then Pete summarized the whole thing. "Guys, this case is wrapped up. We've got an eyewitness account—Jim saw the accident. We've got pictures of the car. And we've got pictures of Senator Dunlap, even with his bloody cheek. When my dad gets all this, they'll have this case closed in a day!"

"How about if we go to your dad's office now?" asked Sam.

"Sounds like a good plan to me," responded Pete.

Chris led the way, saying, "Ringers, this day goes down in the books as one of our all-time best! Wait'll we tell my mom!"

THE END
Turn to page 120.

Pete answered his own question before anyone else had a chance. "Well, I don't see that there's really an option here."

"There isn't?" Chris was getting ready to tease Pete. "Then why'd you even ask us, you nimrod!" Then Chris broke into his imitation of Pete, which he did very well. "Oh gee, fellas. Whadya think we oughta do here?"

In fact, Chris's imitation of Pete sounded exactly like his imitation of Eeyore from *Winnie-the-Pooh*. "Well, just in case you got some ideas, there aren't any possible solutions but mine."

As usual, everyone but Pete was cracking up. And as usual, Pete couldn't care less. He was busy *thinking*. "We have to tell the police."

"Tell the police?" Chris objected. "Come on! What would we say?" At this point Chris pretended he was telling an officer their story. "Uh, gee, officer, us little kids was spying on this couple, and uh, you see, they had a little disagreement, and the lady took something from the man and left. Don't you think you should put out an all-points bulletin?"

Pete went on ignoring Chris in addition to continuing with his logic.

"Listen, my dad has told me over and over not to be afraid to tell the police if I think I see something happening that isn't right. Maybe they will think that we're just kids, but maybe not. We could even help somebody!" He paused to catch his breath, then added, "Besides, aren't Christians supposed to be people who care enough to help others?"

With this statement he walked away from the gang toward a mounted policeman and told him the whole story.

Turn to page 66.

26

A shiver of fear went through Sam. But he was so excited about using his camera to solve this crime that he pushed his fear aside. "Guys, help for the lady should be on the way. I say we go to the Health building before that scum has a chance to get away."

Pete agreed. "Yeah, if we go to the alley first, he could be gone by the time we get to the Health building. Then we wouldn't have any evidence of who he is."

Willy wasn't so easily convinced. "Just what do you propose we do if we find him—try a citizen's arrest?"

"Of course not, Will," answered Sam. "We use this puppy." Sam tapped his camera.

Willy sighed, "Whatever." That meant he would go along with whatever the gang wanted to do, even if he didn't really like the idea.

"Then it's decided," concluded Chris. "Off to the Health building we go!"

CHOICE

Turn to page 112.

The mood was heavy. Everyone wanted to be the first to solve the riddle. But no one wanted to guess wrong. Pete always made people look like idiots when they guessed wrong. It was the only time when he could really tease the others.

An idea popped into Chris's mind, and he decided to give it a shot. "Well, I know I'm setting myself up for complete humiliation, but I've got an idea."

"We're waiting," Pete challenged.

"First you gotta promise not to say anything other than no if I'm wrong. Promise?" Chris wanted assurance that Pete wouldn't tease him.

"OK, OK, what's your answer?"

Chris started slowly, "I'm sure this probably isn't the right answer, but I think maybe it has something to do with West Point, the army academy. It's 'cause you talked about the point, and I know the president didn't go there, so . . ."

As he spoke, Chris became more and more convinced that he wasn't even close to being right. He was very glad he made Pete promise not to tease him.

Pete kept his promise. Quietly, he said, "No."

28

CHOICE ⇒

This was a pretty goofy answer, don't you think? Maybe you should turn back to page 68 and try a different solution.

Looking at each other, Sam and Willy knew they had to say something. It didn't matter what the consequences were—they just couldn't go through with something they knew was wrong.

Chip was the first to notice their hesitation. "Uh-oh, I think our pals are getting cold feet."

John stuck his face right in Sam's and sneered, "Is there a problem, girls?"

"Well . . . uh . . . ," Sam stammered, "we . . . uh . . or at least I don't think," his dry throat swallowed involuntarily, "this is something I should be doing."

Willy was quick to jump in to save his drowning friend.

"Yeah. We just don't believe it's right—"

Randy cut him off before he could finish his sentence. "Don't preach at us, you little twirp!" He looked at John and Chip and said, "I knew these two would wimp out. Let's get out of here!"

Much to Sam and Willy's surprise, the three boys walked off muttering under their breath. A tidal wave of relief swept over both boys. They were in complete shock that they were still in one piece after opposing the older boys. They looked at each other and smiled.

"Sam," Willy broke the silence, "we were wrong to ever go with those guys in the first place. I'm not trying to

30

preach to you like they said we were doing. I was just as wrong as you were." Sam was nodding his head in agreement with everything Willy said—especially the last part.

Sam added, "Hey, I'm glad we stopped when we did. But I think we need to ask God to forgive us and thank him for saving our lives!"

"You're right," Willy agreed with a strange tone in his voice. It was a combination of guilt and relief.

With Willy leading the way, the boys walked back to the Common and sat on one of the park benches. After a moment, Willy looked up into the branches of the tree over their heads and said, "God, I'm sorry I went along partway with something I knew was wrong. Please forgive me. Help me to speak up sooner." He trailed off to give Sam a chance to pray.

"Father," began Sam, "please forgive me, too. I just know this camera can be used for good things, and that's how I want to use it. Oh, and thanks for my friend Willy. Amen."

"In Jesus' name, amen," echoed Willy with a big smile on his face. Together the boys headed back to the Freeze to continue their talk about good uses for the new camera.

CHOICE

Turn to page 68.

Sam thought for a second. He was very frustrated with Chris right now and really didn't want to let him use the camera. And it looked as if he was on the verge of seeing something incredible happen through the lens.

Chris could tell Sam was hesitating. Usually Sam would have said yes right away. But Chris knew this was a time of testing for him. The guys weren't fully trusting him yet.

He rephrased his question. "Can I look next, when you're done?"

That sounded a lot more logical to Sam. In fact, it gave him the first positive feelings about Chris he'd had in the last couple of hours. "Sure, buddy. Just give me one more minute."

Sam's forgiving tone broke the tension. Everyone suddenly felt a bit more comfortable; a bit more relaxed. Just as sure as it had begun, the silent treatment toward Chris ended, and the atmosphere returned to normal.

The collective thoughts of the group were interrupted by Sam's gasp. "Fight!"

"What?" someone asked.

"They're fighting! The man and woman are fighting!"

"You already told us that," Willy objected.

Without moving the camera one centimeter, Sam started into a play-by-play of what he was watching. "No, before it was just verbal. Now they're . . . ooh! . . . She just biffed him in the chest. . . . Whoa! . . . He slapped her right in the face!"

Everyone's eyes were glued on Sam as if he himself were the action. "Oh man! I think she just ended it! She just kicked him really hard! He's lying on the ground, and she's walking away."

"Should we do anything?" Pete wondered out loud.

"I don't know. The guy's just lying there, not moving."

Pete purposely addressed the other guys again. "Really, what do you guys think? What should we do?"

CHOICE ⇒

If the guys decide the fight is none of their business, turn to page 64.

If they decide to tell a policeman, turn to page 12.

If they run over to help the guy, turn to page 15.

"**W**e gotta!" argued Willy. "This is like the ultimate adventure. Do we really have a choice?"

"And that poor lady," Jim insisted, "she deserves some justice. Maybe we can get it for her!"

Sam was scared, but the mood was electric. And it seemed like everyone else wanted to go. He wasn't about to let Chris start teasing him or accusing him of being a wimp. "Let's go," he added with false enthusiasm.

Pete knew the way well, and the guys were soon headed toward the Health building. Before they went inside, they found the man's car and took pictures of it.

They worked hard to remember what detectives would want. The only basis they had for this information was their collective exposure to TV cop shows. They made sure they got a good, clear picture of the license plate, the dented fender, and a bloody handkerchief on the dashboard.

They stood in the main lobby wondering what to do next. The building was enormous—they just didn't know where to start.

"I know where to start," offered Sam.

"Where?"

"In the bathroom."

"The bathroom? Don't be a dork! Why would we look in the bathroom?"

"Well, . . . I gotta use it."

"Oh," said Chris. "That seems like a good enough reason." The whole gang headed laughing for the closest rest room.

As soon as they walked in the door, Jim stopped, causing all four boys behind him to slam into his back.

"Stink! What are you doing, Jim?"

Jim turned around, whispering, "It's him."

Over at the sink a man in an expensive suit was wiping blood off his jacket with a paper towel. On his cheek was a fresh cut. The man!

CHOICE ⟱

Whoa! Massive stress! The gang stumbled onto the man from the accident without even trying. If they panic and start freaking out, turn to page 93.

If they somehow maintain their composure and proceed with a logical plan to get his picture, turn to page 50.

After a minute of laughter, the officer hushed them. Someone was talking to him over his walkie-talkie. He turned his head, and the guys couldn't make out what was being said. All they heard was the sentence: "Well, notify the *Post*. These kids deserve their pictures in the paper."

Chris turned to Pete. "Did he say 'pictures in the paper'?"

The officer turned back and explained. "Well, boys, you've done a great thing for the city of Washington, D.C., today."

"We have?" Sam said.

"Yes. The man you saw is a drug dealer. In fact, he's pretty big-time. We've known about him for a long time but haven't been able to arrest him because we've never had evidence."

Sam was dying to get the whole story. "We gave you evidence?"

"Well, kind of," said the officer in kind tones. "The officer who checked on him recognized him immediately, searched him good, and found enough drugs on him to put him away for a long time. His little ring of pushers is going to have to do some scrambling, and that'll just make it easier for us to catch them too."

"Wow!" Jim couldn't believe it.

Soon a van from a local news station showed up,

followed by other vehicles from each of the local stations and the newspapers. It wasn't often that the city got treated to a story about young kids putting the heat on drug dealers. "Special," one reporter called this story.

That night the excited boys watched themselves on the news at Chris's house ("Pinch me," Sam kept saying; "Gladly," Willy kept replying). They all teased each other about how stupid they looked.

The next day a picture of the whole gang was in the newspaper. They bought several copies and cut out pictures for each one of them, putting them up on the wall in their rooms.

The Ringers remembered that day for a long time—not just because they had a cool adventure but because they'd had a part in putting a drug dealer in jail.

THE END

Turn to page 120.

Pete whispered to the guys, "No one say anything." He pointed to the door.

The gang followed his lead and quietly left the cafeteria. In fact, they kept walking until they were outside the building.

Pete explained, "Look, this is too big. The guy's a senator. Are we really ready to end his career? Are we ready to risk what could happen to us if we accuse him of this? And if we do accuse him, what if we're wrong?"

Willy quickly agreed. "I never thought this would be dangerous. And we need to be careful about throwing around accusations that could ruin someone's life."

Jim was frustrated. "Ruin someone's life? What about that poor old lady? Wasn't her life ruined?"

"But Jim, are you *that* sure he was the man?"

"Yeah. I followed his car."

"But the car could've been someone else's. We don't really know whose car it was."

Sam joined in the conversation. "I guess Pete's right. We need to be pretty careful about how we treat this situation."

The gang agreed to turn the film and the information over to Pete's dad.

And while Pete's dad believed them and did what he could, the result wasn't very satisfying to any of the guys.

38

They never heard anything more about the lady. Nor did anything ever happen to the senator. Pete's dad told them not to be discouraged, but it was hard to follow his advice.

As far as the Ringers could tell, the world stayed pretty much the way it was before they came down from the Washington Monument and searched for a hit-and-run driver.

THE END

Turn to page 120.

Sam looked at the ground for a few seconds. Slowly he said, "I'm sorry, Willy. I'm a little bit nervous about this camera 'cause I know how much it must have cost. But I know you'll be careful with it if anyone will." A small smile crept over his face, and then he launched into his best gangster voice, "Besides, Buster, if you drop it, I'll kill ya!"

Willy leaned over with a hearty laugh. "*You* kill *me?* Ha!"

Sam's smile melted into one of pride as he cautiously handed the camera over to Willy.

Willy couldn't believe what he saw through the lens. "You really can see forever," he said with a gasp. "We gotta figure out a place where we can really test this out. I mean, this thing is like the ultimate spy tool. We could use it to check out some stuff we couldn't usually see."

"Yeah, like Pete kissing his mom good-night!"

Both boys erupted into laughter. Their friend Pete was a good guy, but he was a little clumsy sometimes. Not that Sam and Willy didn't kiss their moms good-night— they just liked teasing Pete about anything they could think of.

Just as their laughter was dying down, three older boys walked out of the Freeze and over to where they were sitting. Sam and Willy had seen the boys around town and knew they were trouble.

"Hey little boy, got a new toy there?" one of the boys teased.

Sam said nothing. These boys could cause them a lot of grief if they wanted to, and Sam wasn't about to smart back at them.

Another said, "Hey, that's actually a pretty nice camera. I bet we could see all the way into Ronda Turner's bedroom window with that."

"Yeah!" agreed the third, "from the window in my attic."

"*While* she's changing!" the second boy added.

"Sounds like a plan to me," confirmed the first boy. He turned to Sam and Willy. "I know we're not usually very nice to you, but this could be the start of a brand new friendship." All three older boys snickered.

Sam looked at Willy. Neither of them had said a single word since the older boys approached them. Neither of them wanted to say anything now either. But the same thoughts were running through their mind. These boys might be pretty fun to hang around with. They were very popular in school. It would be great to know some older guys when Sam and Willy got to high school. And Ronda Turner was very pretty.

CHOICE ⟹

If Sam and Willy go with the boys, turn to page 53.

If Sam says something against going with the boys, turn to page 72.

If Willy thinks they should go and Sam doesn't, turn to page 83.

42

Jim panicked. He was so scared he started talking very fast in Portuguese, the language he had learned in Brazil.

The man stopped. He wasn't sure how to respond. After a couple of seconds he snapped, "Shut that kid up and give me my stuff!"

"No!" Chris gained his composure and said defiantly.

"No?"

"That's right, I said no. There's a lot more of us than you, and we're not going to give you those awful drugs."

The man laughed and imitated Chris in a old lady's voice: "We're not gonna give you those awful drugs." Then his voice dropped as fast as his smile disappeared. "Oh yeah?"

The boys all realized at that moment that the man had pulled a switchblade knife out of his pocket and was holding it toward them at his waist.

No one said a word. Instead, they all ran—in different directions.

Jim was all alone, running with the drugs in his hand, followed closely by the drug man. Jim was screaming at the top of his lungs.

People were watching them from every direction. A mounted policeman galloped his horse over between Jim and the man and stopped them both.

The drug man looked around frantically but didn't

run away. He began to whimper pitifully, hunched over like a disobedient dog, pacing unsteadily in a rough circle.

The other boys stopped running and headed for Jim, the drug man, and the mounted policeman as Jim blurted out the whole story in one long, fast sentence. "We watched this guy get in a fight through a camera then we came to see if he was OK and I found these drugs on the ground and he told me to give 'em to him and I didn't and he threatened me with a knife and I ran then you showed up just in time and I can't believe it I'm scared Mr. Officer! Here." Jim held out the drugs to the officer, who was now off his horse putting handcuffs on the drug man.

The end result was "pretty cool," as Willy put it. The whole gang took a ride down to the police station and gave official testimonies about the incident.

They found out that the man was wanted for drug dealing but that the police hadn't been able to catch him with drugs on him. Thanks to Jim, now they had.

Despite the excitement, it scared the guys to think how close they had gotten to a real live drug dealer.

"Whose idea was this trip to D.C. thing, anyway?" Chris asked half-jokingly.

"Doesn't matter," answered Jim. "Trips into the city *never* go the way we plan."

"You can say *that* again," added Sam.

"Yeah, especially with *you* along," said Willy.

Yet another oh yeah?–yeah!–oh yeah?–yeah! battle erupted. Both sides suffered heavy giggle casualties before making their rendezvous with Chris's mom.

44

THE END

Turn to page 120.

All four boys remained completely silent as they struggled to figure out the riddle. Pete was quite happy with himself and had a humongous grin on his face.

Sam sat up straight on the bench and spoke in a proper British accent. "By jove, I think I've got it!"

"Well, let's hear it," Pete challenged. The other three boys nodded in agreement.

"OK, you said there's a great view from the point. And people often say, 'There's a great view from the top,' meaning the boss or person in charge. And you mentioned the president. So you must be talking about the White House. Yeah, you want us to go spying in the White House."

Chris and Willy were nodding in agreement. Jim looked like he wasn't convinced.

"Ha!" Pete didn't have to say much to shatter Sam's hopes of being the one to solve the riddle. "You should have guessed *your* house, since you're the president of all point heads."

CHOICE ⇒

Obviously this was the wrong choice. Turn to page 68 and try again.

By the time the guys got to the park, they were totally out of breath.

"This was a great idea, Willy!" snipped Chris sarcastically.

"It wasn't my idea!" Willy said, defensively. "I think it was Jim's."

"What are you talking about?" reacted Jim. "I was the last one to know we were even going anywhere. I had to catch up to *you* guys."

No one was sure whose idea it had been. But by now it didn't matter—they were only about fifteen feet from the man. They had passed the woman as she was hurriedly getting on a bus.

"Hey, mister," Chris called. "Are you OK? We saw that lady kick you and take some stuff from you. Do you want us to get a policeman?"

The man smiled very painfully. "Police? You don't have to call the police." He slowly reached inside his coat pocket and pulled out a badge. "I *am* the police." He tried to get up but groaned and fell back. That's when the kids saw he was bleeding from his side.

"Hey," said Pete, "that woman wasn't taking something from him. She was knifing him! We've really got to get help, now."

Sam was the first to spot the mounted policeman

riding about a hundred yards away. He bolted in that direction, shouting at the top of his lungs, "Help! Help!"

The officer heard and spotted him right away and wheeled his horse in Sam's direction. Sam was gesturing wildly and running beside the galloping horse as they came back. The policeman was already using his hand radio to call for an ambulance when he rode up.

"Thanks, boys, for getting involved," he said as he dismounted and took a first-aid kit from his saddlebag. "You've probably saved this officer's life!" He pulled out some thick bandages and used them to stop the bleeding. The boys found it hard to look.

The wounded man had been lying still, but he groaned again and opened his eyes. "Don't make me laugh," he said quietly. "I know that will hurt even more than it does now."

The other officer told him to keep still because help was on the way. As if on cue, the siren from an ambulance sounded in the distance. When the wounded policeman had been taken away, the mounted policeman turned to the boys. "I want to thank you boys again for helping my fellow officer. I'm sure you could tell he was working undercover. We know there are several major drug dealers using the Mall as an exchange point. One of the most notorious is this woman you saw knife the officer. Did you get a good look at her?"

"I think we can do better than that," said Sam with one of his lobe to lobe smiles. "I took at least two pictures of her!" He held up his camera proudly.

Those turned out to be the magic words. Moments

later the boys were being taken by squad car to a police station, where they got an interesting tour while Sam's film was being developed in the lab. They even got to check out the lab, although the darkroom was so small that Sam was the only one of the gang who got to go in there.

Everyone crowded around when the technician brought out the photos. "Hey, kid. You could get a job around here with that camera," he said, speaking to Sam. The pictures had turned out crystal clear. One just showed a man and woman having a conversation. The other distinctly showed a knife in her hand pointed in the direction of the officer.

"He never saw it coming," said one of the policemen who was with them. "But when we catch her, these pictures will help a lot to put her away."

The boys were amazed at the number of policemen who had heard about their actions and stopped them in the hall to say thanks. Before the gang left the station they were told that the officer they had helped had been operated on and was going to be fine. The officer who drove them to meet Chris's mom told them that because this incident involved an undercover operation that was still going on, they would have to be sworn to secrecy.

The boys sat crammed five across in the backseat of the squad car looking at each other. Could the Ringers keep a secret? You better believe it!

Several weeks later, a well-dressed young man walked into the Freeze. He sat at the counter for a while, watching and listening while the Ringers goofed around in their favorite booth. They didn't notice him until he walked over toward them. "Hello, boys," he said. When he realized they didn't recognize him, he said, "Now, don't call the police—because I *am* the police!"

They all had a good laugh over that one. The officer introduced himself as Tom Weeks. He had stopped by to thank the boys personally. They were glad to see he was well.

"I'm sorry you guys won't be public heroes over this," said Tom. "It's one of the prices you pay when you do undercover work. But you're real heroes in my book. You saved my life. We haven't caught that woman yet, but she hasn't stopped dealing, so its only a matter of time. Thanks for giving me a second chance!" He shook hands warmly with each of the boys and then left.

No sooner had the door closed than Betty, the owner and ice cream magician at the Freeze, approached the booth and announced, "I don't know what you boys did to deserve this, but I've been instructed to let you each order whatever you want today. So, go for it!"

The boys sat stunned for a moment. Then Sam lifted his hand in the traditional high-five invitation and yelled, "Who said undercover work doesn't pay off!"

THE END
Turn to page 120.

Chris spoke quietly through his lips without moving them—like a ventriloquist whispering. "Stay calm. No one freak out. Everyone spread out and try to act normal. Sam, get a picture of him."

As if they had planned and practiced this hundreds of times, they all responded correctly. Willy calmly walked over to the hand dryer and smoothly pretended to dry his already-dry hands. Pete went to a mirror and started to comb his hair.

Sam took position right behind a little divider between the man and the rest of the bathroom. Once he got the camera ready, he counted to three in his mind. Then he jumped out next to the man and snapped a picture.

"What?" the man said, startled, as he spun around to face Sam.

"Thanks," Sam answered quickly. With that he walked quickly toward the door. Everyone followed him, with the man close on the gang's heels.

Outside the rest room the man caught up to Sam and gently grabbed his shoulder.

Sam's heart leapt. Visions of this man pulverizing him right there in the hallway of the Health and Human Services building ran through his head.

"Young man," the man started calmly, "why did you take a picture of the back of my head?"

Chris looked at Sam in amazement. "Yeah, why did you take a picture of the back of his head?" he said, forgetting the gravity of the situation. Right now he was more concerned that Sam took a worthless photo than that the man might strangle Sam.

"I . . . I . . ." Sam stuttered, expecting the man to feed him his camera any second.

"If you want my photo, all you have to do is ask," he said with a smile.

Sam blinked in shock. A small grain of logic leaked out of his scrambled mind, wobbled to his mouth, and limply presented itself to a waiting world: "May I take your picture?"

All eyes zoomed to the man.

"Well, of course you can!" The man straightened himself, showing not a hint of hit-and-run guilt.

Sam numbly focused his camera as the man adjusted his suit and tie and stood tall beside one of the paintings on the wall.

Chris, Pete, and Jim watched silently in amazement, paralyzed by this man's unexpected behavior. How could a hit-and-run driver be so nice? Finally suspicious, Chris was the first to come out of his coma. "Take a few to make sure we have a good one, Sam."

"Right." Sam took four pictures of the smiling man.

Then the man shook their hands and walked off.

The dazed group formed a circle, as if someone had called a meeting.

52

"Too weird!" said Willy.

"No kidding!" Jim agreed.

"What do we do now?" asked Jim.

"Develop the film!" said Chris.

With their work complete, the gang headed for home.

Days later, after Pete's dad got the film developed, they found out why the man was so friendly and photogenic. What a shock!

THE END

If you're ready for a shock of your own, turn to page 93.

Both Sam and Willy knew they shouldn't go with the older boys—for lots of reasons. They knew the boys were just using them. They knew their own parents would ground them for life if they went along with the proposal. And they knew spying on a girl in her bedroom, especially while she was changing, was a sin.

But for some reason—a reason neither of them could explain later—they both said OK at the same time. And before they knew it, they were walking toward Ronda Turner's house with the three high school boys.

They soon learned the boys' names were John, Randy, and Chip. John was short, but seemed like the leader of the group. Chip was very quiet. And Randy was a live wire; he almost hopped instead of walking and kept reviewing the plan as they moved down the sidewalk. They were all headed for his attic.

"This is great! It's Tuesday morning, so both my parents are at work," Randy babbled. "I can see Ronda's window from my house, but it's just too far away to see the good stuff."

No one else really talked, so Randy just continued gabbing. "And I know her schedule like the back of my hand. Every morning she has breakfast with her family around eight o'clock. Then she sits in her bedroom and

. . ." Randy paused, then spoke slowly in a low, spooky voice: "Then, get this, she reads her Bible."

Both Sam and Willy felt chills.

Chip mumbled, "I thought you said you couldn't see very well. How do you know she's reading her Bible?"

"Hey, I just know, OK?" was Randy's answer. He suddenly stopped all the boys by jumping in front of them on the sidewalk. They were all a bit surprised and stared at him, waiting for something.

Slowly a huge grin swept over Randy's face. After a couple seconds of this dumb-looking smile, he quietly said, "And then . . . she takes off her pajamas for her shower."

John and Chip went wild and starting giving each other high fives like football players in the end zone.

Willy glanced over at Sam and their eyes met for the first time since they had agreed to go along. Both were feeling guilty like crazy, but neither had the guts to say something at that moment. Their stomachs were doing acrobatic loops.

CHOICE ⇒

If Sam and Willy change their minds and don't go with the boys, turn to page 29.

If neither boy says anything and they continue with John, Randy, and Chip, turn to page 20.

Sam's reaction caught Willy completely off guard.

"No stinkin' way! Not a chance!" he shot off. "I just got this two hours ago, and it's the most expensive thing I own. You'd probably bust it."

Willy was shocked. One of his best friends was treating him like a little kid. For what seemed like a long time, he just sat there with his mouth hanging open. He wasn't sure how he should react.

Finally his anger got the best of him. "Well, fine! Man, I can't believe what an idiot you're being. Keep your stupid camera to yourself; and while you're at it, keep your friendship to yourself."

Willy defiantly stood up from the rough cement bench and walked away.

Sam just sat there alone, staring at his camera.

THE END

If you don't want a Ringers adventure to end like this, turn back to page 1 and make a different choice.

56

The gang made its way down the main hallway of the Health building.

"I wonder what they do here at this place?" wondered Willy aloud.

"Well," began Pete, "it's called the Department of Health and Human Services—"

"I know," interrupted Sam. "It'd be a great service to humanity if they'd send Willy to the moon!"

"I think they should send *you* instead," Chris said to Sam. "But c'mon. Let's get serious. We've got a criminal to find!"

"Lead on, O Brazilian One!" Sam teased Jim.

Jim made some comment in Portuguese that nobody understood. Sam decided he didn't want to find out what it meant.

The guys started carefully looking over the people—especially men in suits. Jim glanced around more quickly because he could recognize the man's face. The other boys tried to find a scuffed cheek.

After about twenty minutes of looking, everyone was bored.

"This stinks!" Chris said, flustered.

"It doesn't smell over here," Sam teased. "There's a bathroom down the hall if you need it."

Willy and Jim burst into giggles.

"Ha, ha, ha," Chris said dryly. "Seriously, I'm bored."

"Hi, Bored, I'm Sam. Nice to meet you."

"Would you cut that out?" Chris was getting frustrated.

"Sure, just hand me a knife."

"Argh!" Chris lunged at Sam and pretended to strangle him. Sam responded by offering loud fake gagging sounds.

"Shhhhh!" An official-looking man poked his head out of a doorway and glared at the boys.

Sam and Chris both pointed at each other in an attempt to transfer blame. Doing this at the exact same time made them laugh even harder. Sam even started snorting like a pig—something he did only when he really couldn't control his laughter.

The snorting sound made Willy and Jim laugh. And soon even Pete was doubled over roaring.

The man stormed over to them, grabbed Chris by the collar, and said, "This building is no place for horseplay. You troublemakers will leave at once, or I'll be forced to call security!"

Sam felt bad about making the man angry. "I'm sorry, sir. We didn't mean to cause any trouble."

"Apology not accepted," the man snapped. "Leave at once!"

The boys shuffled toward the exit, still amusing themselves with occasional giggle bursts.

Once outside, Pete said, "Well, it was still a cool adventure, even though we didn't find the guy."

"Yeah," agreed Sam, "if only Chris hadn't gone crazy!"

Instantly, Chris was at Sam's throat, pretending to

58

strangle him again, and the laughter began all over again. Being caught up in the fun made them kind of forget about catching criminals. Their afternoon was gone before they knew it, and they missed finding the man they had set out to catch.

THE END

Making other choices could have made a big difference—you might even help the guys find the man! Turn back to page 112 and make different choices.

Or, turn to page 120.

Everything went smoothly, and by 12:30 the boys were on the Mall in Washington, D.C. Chris's mom had ridden down with them on the subway, and in a rare moment of leniency she allowed them to go off on their own if they agreed to meet her at the station by 6:00. They now had the Washington Monument in sight.

"Let's get cookin'!" Sam was pumped about the excitement over his new camera. He was enjoying being the center of attention.

Pete echoed Sam's impatience with, "Now it's up the Washington Monument. You guys all brought a few bucks for the admission fee, right?"

"Yeah," came the response from all but Jim.

"Admission fee? You guys didn't say anything about an admission fee."

Sam spoke up, "We didn't think we needed to. You're the one with all the knowledge about the Washington Monument, Mr. Riddle-solver."

"Give me a break! We didn't exactly get quizzed on the admission fees of various sites in the U.S. capital." Jim was enjoying the verbal boxing match between himself and Sam. All the other boys had learned long ago that they could never win in teasing battles with Sam. But Jim was still new enough to get away with it.

"Well," Pete said, concentrating on the money issue

and ignoring the teasing, "how much extra money do you guys have? I'm sure we have enough to cover him if we put it all into a pool."

Sam turned his teasing toward Pete. "Won't he get wet when he tries to get the money out?"

Everyone groaned except Pete. He continued, "I've got fifty cents left after I set aside my return subway fare."

"I've got a buck extra," Sam offered.

"I'm sorry," Willy apologized. "I only brought enough money for my fare and admission."

Pete looked at Chris, who did not look back. "Chris, what about you? We'll probably need a little more to cover Jim. You got it?"

"Oh, man," Chris started with about five tons of reservation in his voice. "I've got three bucks extra."

"So what's the problem?" Pete questioned.

Chris sighed loudly and dropped his shoulders. "I've been waiting for six months to buy a George Washington squirt pen."

"A *what?*" Pete asked with disbelief.

"A George Washington squirt pen. It's great. It looks just like a normal pen with a picture of George Washington and some other historical stuff printed on the side. But the cool thing is, it's not really a pen; it's a miniature squirt gun. It's one of the funniest pranks I've ever seen. And I've been saving for it since the first time I saw it." He paused. "And it costs two dollars and fifty cents."

"So let me get this right." Pete said in his data-processing mode. "You're gonna buy a little squirt gun, which means we won't have enough money for Jim to go up in the monument."

Jim was uncomfortable because things were getting hot between Chris and Pete, and it was all because he hadn't thought to bring enough money. "Hey, don't worry about it guys. I can wait at the bottom until you come back down. It's no big deal."

"Sure it's a big deal," said Pete in defense of Jim. "We're talking about a squirt gun here."

Now it was Chris's turn to get defensive. "Wait a minute. I never said I wouldn't lend him the money."

"So you will?" Pete pressed for an answer.

CHOICE ➡

If Chris decides to loan Jim the money, turn to page 87.

If Chris decides to buy his squirt pen instead of lending Jim the money, turn to page 74.

Jim had no idea what to do. In desperation he threw the bag at the man, hitting him right in the face. The bag burst open, covering the man's face with white powder.

Jim shrieked and stepped aside to avoid getting bowled over.

"You little idiot!" the man exploded at Jim. "I said, 'Give it to me,' not 'Throw it at me'!" He wiped the powder off his face and stood up for the first time. "You just wasted five hundred dollars' worth of cocaine! And you're gonna *pay* for it!"

The man lunged again toward Jim. But Pete stuck out his foot and tripped the man, sending him sprawling on the ground once more.

Instantly all five boys broke into a sprint. They ran until they realized the man had stopped chasing them.

When they finally came to a stop, they looked back to see the drug man kneeling on the ground.

"Sam, take a picture of him," Willy suggested.

Sam pulled out his camera and focused the big lens. "He's trying to pick up the powder out of the grass, but it looks like he's not doing very well."

Sam snapped three shots before putting the camera back into its bag. "Later we can develop the film and give the pictures to the police." The others silently agreed.

The gang tried to find an officer right then, but before they could, the drug man ran off.

This sure wasn't the kind of adventure they had envisioned for their day. But it gave them lots to talk about for the rest of the summer.

THE END

Turn to page 120.

"**H**ey," Willy began, "this is none of our business. We probably shouldn't have been watching them anyway."

"I agree with Willy," Pete said.

The entire gang seemed a little relieved—except Sam. He really wanted an adventure to center on his camera. But the next idea that came up dissolved that concern.

"I know!" It was Chris, back to his normal self. "There are other ways to have fun with a camera than to spy on people. You do have film in that thing, don't you?"

"Yeah."

"Well, how 'bout using it to take some of the goofiest pictures ever taken in the history of the world?"

A chorus of yeahs erupted. Everyone loved Chris's idea.

The Ringers spent the rest of their afternoon taking pictures that could go in a book of world records under the title "Goofiest Group Pictures." They got a shot of Willy, Chris, and Jim on the back of a police horse, with the policeman still on it—four people on one horse! They took a picture of Pete, Sam, and Willy doing ballet poses on the steps of the Smithsonian Institution. Then there was the one with everyone but Pete (he took the picture) having a pretend sword fight with the George Washington squirt pens they all purchased from a souvenir shop. Even Chris got a chuckle out of that one—because Jim won the sword fight with the pen that Chris had bought for him.

But their favorite one wasn't even funny. It was just a picture of the whole gang standing by the base of the Lincoln Memorial. They had asked a worker to take the picture for them. Later they all got a copy of that one, and most of the guys stuck it up in their room somewhere.

They accomplished exactly what they had set out to do that day. No, they hadn't had much of an adventure with the camera. But they had used it to have a fun time together. And that's all the Ringers really wanted—to enjoy the friends God had given them.

THE END

If you haven't met the senator yet, turn to page 59 and make different choices along the way.

Or, turn to page 120.

In response to Pete's story, the officer spoke into a walkie-talkie, directing several other police on the Mall to check out the man.

When the officers approached him, he ran. They chased him on foot, and a police helicopter that happened to be in the area cut the guy off so the pursuers could catch him. The Ringers waited with the policeman while he monitored the chase on his radio. It was over quickly.

"You boys have done Washington, D.C., a great service today," the officer said. "We've been trying to catch this guy for a long time."

"Who is he?" several of the boys asked at once.

"A drug dealer," the officer replied simply. The guys whistled.

Several minutes later, the helicopter pilot asked the gang, "How about as a reward, we give you boys a little tour of the city from the air?"

The guys couldn't believe their ears. Helicopters were so cool, and they had actually been offered a free ride!

"Of course we'd like a ride!" Chris answered.

"Mega-yes!" added Sam.

"Let's go then."

All five boys scrambled into the door of the helicopter with huge smiles on their faces. This was the ultimate!

The helicopter slowly lifted off the ground, then gently moved out over the massive city.

The view was beautiful, and they could see everything: the Washington Monument and the Capitol building, the Lincoln Memorial, the White House, the Air and Space Museum. They could even see far down the Potomac River. They could see Millersburg off in the distance. Willy was even sure he could see his apartment building.

Sam used the camera to take some fantastic pictures. Later, each of the guys got copies for their scrapbooks.

All in all, it turned out to be quite an adventurous day—and they never did make it up the Washington Monument!

THE END

Turn to page 120.

The day was much too nice to stay inside, so Sam and Willy went and sat under a tree in the Common and started working on their triple-scoop ice cream cones. The cones were melting fast in the summer heat and required a lot of attention.

Both boys were trying hard to think of fun ways to use the new camera. Neither was coming up with much.

"Hey, dweebs!"

Sam and Willy were happy to look up and see Pete, Chris, and Jim—more of the Ringers. Something fun was sure to happen now.

"What's up?" Chris was poking around the black camera bag, trying to find out what was inside without actually asking or opening it. He was the unofficial leader of their group; or at least he often took that role.

Pete was tall and goofy looking. The guys teased him a lot, but he was usually a good sport about it.

Jim was one of the recent members of the Ringers. He and his sister, Tina, had just moved to Millersburg from Brazil, where their parents were missionaries. They were living with their grandparents now so they could go to school in the States.

Willy took a quick break from his cone to slurp out, "You shud shee wa Sham gah—iz sho coo!" He swallowed and continued, "Show 'em, Sam."

"OK, but I don't want to get ice cream all over it. That would really mess it—"

"Stop gabbing and show us!" Chris interrupted. He was frustrated in anticipation.

Sam smiled real big and pulled the camera out of its bag.

"Awesome!" Pete jumped forward to look closer. "That's a great camera! And check out that lens—it's got to be at least a 500mm."

"Exactly," responded Sam with pride in his voice.

Pete knew tons about anything and everything technical. He could take apart almost any electronic device and put it back together again.

Willy said, "We've been trying to think of something fun we can do to really test out its spy-ability. You can almost see California with this thing. But we can't come up with anything—other than looking at Jim's grandpa at the church."

Jim's eyes lit up. "You can see that far? Can I see?"

"You'll all get a chance to try it out, but only after we come up with an adventure. This is too nice a day, and too nice a camera, to waste spying on the church." Sam wanted to get going now that his cone was gone and all the boys were there.

Pete spoke up. "How 'bout D.C.?"

"You mean go into the city? What could we do there?" Sam wasn't convinced.

Pete winked and answered, "I've got a great idea, but you'll have to figure it out."

"Oh, man," Chris groaned. "Not another riddle!"

Pete was very smart, and he loved to get back at the guys for their teasing by making them figure out riddles. Only Jim seemed to like them, but he hadn't been around very long.

"What's the riddle?" said Jim. The others were still rolling their eyes.

Pete spoke slowly and clearly, as you'd speak to someone who barely knows English. "This is where we should go: The view from the point is great, but this president's never even seen it."

"What?" Chris hated riddles—or at least pretended to. "That doesn't make any sense. You probably don't even have an answer. You're just trying to make fools of us."

"Get a clue," Pete came back at Chris, using a pun that only he thought was funny.

The rest of the boys were already thinking, trying to come up with an answer that didn't sound totally stupid.

CHOICE ⟹

If the riddle has something to do with the president in office right now, turn to page 45.

If the answer will be about the first president of the United States, turn to page 107.

If it's about West Point, the army academy, turn to page 27.

If Pete's talking about Mark Newhouse, the point guard on their school basketball team and student government president, turn to page 98.

Sam and Willy sighed at the exact same time, and then they both giggled. It was the kind of laughing sound you make when you're in church and want to laugh but know your parents will make you go to bed early for the next fourteen years if you do.

One of the older boys got impatient and said, "Let's get out of here. We don't need this bonehead's toy to have fun."

Willy decided to be courageous. After all, he didn't think these guys were as tough as they wanted everyone to think they were. "Well, we wouldn't go with you guys anyway. We can find better ways to have fun than by getting arrested as Peeping Toms."

The older boys were surprised Willy had stood up to them. Sam was pretty surprised too. And combined with his giggle remnants, the most he could add was, "Yeah."

"Well . . . ," the leader of the older boys began, fishing for words, "we'll see you Twinkies in high school." It was supposed to be a threat. Sam and Willy just laughed.

After the older boys left, Willy had a great idea. "Hey, making the right choice always makes me hungry!"

"I'm way ahead of you," Sam said as he jumped past Willy and darted into the Freeze.

CHOICE

Turn to page 68.

Chris didn't know how to answer. He wanted the squirt pen a lot. He'd been saving for the chance to get it, and now he had that chance. Why should he feel responsible for Jim's not knowing he had to bring money? Besides, Jim did say he didn't mind waiting at the bottom.

Before long Chris convinced himself that Jim really didn't mind waiting. "Jim?" he asked, quietly. "Since you offered to stay down this time, I really would like to get my pen."

The guys were shocked—first, because they'd never heard Chris talk so politely in their lives; second, because they couldn't believe how selfish he was being.

While everyone stood there blinking in amazement, Jim jumped in with, "That's fine, Chris. I'll just wait right here on this bench."

"It's not like we're gonna be up there all day," Chris added, trying to make the situation brighter. He turned to the other guys and, in an effort to take the attention away from himself, shouted: "Last one to the elevator is a camel carcass!"

Chris took off running toward the monument at full speed.

No one else moved. They all watched Chris run, waiting for him to figure out that they weren't running with him. But he didn't notice, and he didn't look back. He kept charging ahead full speed, obviously thinking he was beating everyone. As he got closer and closer to the monument, the guys started laughing.

Chris kept running.

The gang started cheering him on.

Chris kept running.

The gang went wild, jumping and shouting. Chris was too far away to hear them by now. Finally, he reached the ring of flags around the monument base, turned around, and threw up his arms in victory. It took him a moment to realize he was alone. Way behind he saw his friends waving and pushing each other as they laughed. He also saw himself in a new way, too. Pete had been right. A squirt pen definitely wasn't worth a friendship. It couldn't even compare. Shaking his head, Chris trotted back toward the group.

Meanwhile, Sam broke the laughter with, "Come on, guys. Let's find something else to do that doesn't cost as much money."

All the guys echoed their approval of Sam's idea. Jim smiled. It was at times like this that he could hardly believe he had such a great group of friends.

The guys began discussing their options.

CHOICE

Turn to page 102.

Chris was a good leader. He took charge well and usually had good ideas. But occasionally his desire to lead and do something overruled his better judgment and caused him to suggest solutions that weren't very well thought out. This was one of those times.

"I've got a better idea," he said.

Mr. Rey looked surprised. "Hey kid, this isn't a debate. Just give me the film."

"We will, but listen to my idea first."

"OK, but make it quick."

"Well, you see, this is the first roll of film we've ever taken with Sam's camera. And there are some pictures of us here in the city that we'd really like to keep. So how about if we pull the roll out of the camera and cut the film in half—you can take the film you want, and we'll keep the film we want."

Chris figured they could give the guy some of the pictures he wanted, but not all of them. They'd keep just enough pictures to prove their point.

Mr. Rey got a big grin on his face. "That sounds like a great idea."

"But, Chris . . . ," Sam began, looking frustrated.

"Sam, don't ask any questions, just do it." Chris couldn't believe how easily his plan was working. He didn't even stop to wonder why Sam would have a problem with it.

Sam was still hesitating, so Chris grabbed the camera and popped the back open. He grabbed the film by the edges and pulled it out of the camera. To his surprise, Mr. Rey began to laugh.

"Sam," Chris said puzzled, "how do you tell which frame is which? It's all just clear."

With that Mr. Rey laughed so hard he doubled over. He spun around and walked out of the rest room, still laughing and shaking his head.

When the door closed, Chris continued under the delusion that he had pulled a major victory with his brilliant plan. He whirled around to face the guys. "This is great! He left us with the whole roll! I can't believe he just left! *Yes!*"

"Why shouldn't he?" Pete questioned. "There's no proof here—"

"What are you talking about?" Chris noticed for the first time that he seemed to be the only one who was excited.

Sam explained with more sadness and disappointment than anger, "Chris, you exposed the film when you opened the back of the camera. There aren't any pictures left on here. That's why I was trying to stop you."

"But—" Chris felt a warm rush pulse through his entire body. "Oh no!" he said, looking down at the film.

Jim could tell Chris was about to cry. "Chris. It's OK. We were in way over our heads anyway. At least you got that guy to leave. Who knows what he might have done to us if you hadn't made him laugh so hard."

"Yeah?" Chris said with some hope in his voice. "I guess you're right, Jim. Anyway, they still might catch him."

"Don't count on it," said Pete. "All the police would have to go on is Jim's testimony that he saw the accident from blocks away—and maybe paint chips from the car. Remember, the rest of us never actually saw the accident. The courts would never accept Jim's testimony without more proof."

That night the guys watched the evening news to see if the accident was reported. But it was just another hit-and-run in a city with thousands of people—the reports made no mention of the poor old lady. However, the news did cover a speech given by Senator Dunlap on the "pressing needs of the less fortunate."

The Ringers had much to think about that night.

THE END

Turn to page 120.

As if it made a bit of difference, all five boys held their breath. Randy even closed his eyes, like a child thinking, *Maybe they won't see me if I can't see them.*

When the car drove on by without stopping, they all let out a huge gasp of air from their lungs. The rush of panic that swept over them had come and gone at approximately the speed of a booster shot—pretty quick, but not fast enough.

The enormous sound of their collective sigh made them all burst out in laughter. This, in turn, caused the four in the attic to collapse to the floor.

Randy, who had been laughing with them, screamed out, "Don't let go of my waist!" But it was too late.

Randy's feet lifted about six inches off the floor before Chip grabbed him. Randy flailed about, launching the camera into the air. In fact, he threw it so high that Sam caught a glimpse of it as it passed the window on its way toward earth.

In the silence following the scream, no one missed the distinct crunching sound of the camera meeting the small square of concrete by the side door to Randy's garage. The camera was a complete loss. As he picked up the shattered lens and twisted metal parts, tears rolled down Sam's face. Breaking the camera was bad enough. It was worse to think about the stupid choices they had made on their way to ruining a very special gift.

Needless to say, any chance of adventure was shot for that day. Sam had a hard time explaining to his uncle Jeff what happened. He also got grounded for three weeks by his parents—on summer vacation, no less.

Willy didn't fare much better. His parents made him give the seventy dollars he had saved so far this year to Sam's uncle to help pay for the camera. They said, "You and Sam bought that camera when you chose to use it in improper ways."

And Willy's thoughts were correct. The next (and last) time Sam and Willy spoke to the boys, they found out that Randy's parents didn't fall for the rock-through-the-window story. Randy had to pay to fix the broken attic window.

They all had to agree that spying on Ronda Turner was a pretty dumb idea in the first place.

THE END

Turn to page 120.

"**W**hat are you guys talking about!" Sam said more than asked. He knew exactly what they meant; he just didn't like it. "We're just kids. We can't go running off to capture some potential criminal." Sam's voice was practically squeaking with disbelief, as if he'd pushed his vocal chords to the top of his throat.

Jim and Chris were quiet. They knew they were asking the guys to do something that was somewhat dangerous. Though Chris was never completely out of words, the most even he could muster was, "Well . . ."

"The police will be looking for the guy," Willy said, siding with Sam. "And Pete, your dad works for the FBI—you know they can find a person even when it's a hit-and-run."

Pete confirmed Willy's statement. "Yeah, they have color matches from every year, make, and model of every car. They'll brush the lady's clothes for any paint chips that got on her during the accident—a person almost always gets paint on him when a car hits him. Then they'll know the guy's exact car color, year, model, and make. It's really cool."

Sam decided it was good timing for a little humor and said, "Pete, if Willy breathes on me, could they scrape my clothes and tell what year he was born?"

Pete jokingly glared at Sam. "I won't even honor that comment with a response, you ninny!"

Willy and Sam looked at each other and said at the same time, *"Ninny?"*

"So we're not gonna do anything?" Jim still wanted an answer.

"How 'bout taking a vote?" Pete was being the mediator. "Even if we don't go, I'll tell my dad, and he can give the police everything we know."

"That makes sense to me," said Willy. "Raise your hand if you think we shouldn't get into this and should just tell Pete's dad."

Everyone raised his hand but Jim.

"Well, it's decided then. That OK with you, Jim?"

"Yeah," Jim said reluctantly.

The rest of the afternoon was weird. The gang tried to have fun and forget what they had seen. But no one could get out of their heads the picture of that old lady being loaded into the ambulance. And Jim would never forget watching a hit-and-run take place.

THE END

If you'd rather catch the guy after all, turn to page 33.

Or, turn to page 120.

Willy was the first to speak. "Yeah, that sounds kinda fun." There was a hint of reservation in his voice.

"What? Are you kidding, Willy?" Sam reacted. "I can't believe it!"

"C'mon, midget," barked one of the older boys. "Your friend's got a good head on his shoulders. Maybe you should follow his advice."

Sam was getting courageous now. Once he had taken a stand, he knew deep down that he was doing the right thing. And he was sure Jesus wouldn't want him using his new camera to watch Ronda Turner change her clothes.

"Give me a break!" he huffed with a disgusted tone of voice. "You can't make me do something I don't want to do. And you better believe you're not going to touch my camera!"

With that Sam walked away from the boys—including Willy. They were all shocked by Sam's swift counterattack. Willy felt ashamed he hadn't spoken up like Sam. He got up and walked after Sam. He knew he would have some apologizing to do.

THE END

It would really be a shame to see an adventure end before it even gets started! Turn to page 39 and make a different choice.

"**F**ood!" said Willy, revealing his preference.

"Willy," Sam started, "even if we do start in the cafeteria, we're not going to get any food. Have you forgotten that we are just about out of money? Besides, we don't have time to goof around."

"Who's goofin' around? I'm hungry."

"OK, Willy, we'll go to the cafeteria. But you have to agree only to buy something cheap you can eat fast."

"Deal!"

With that the gang headed off toward the cafeteria.

Upon arrival, Willy got in line to get an ice cream sandwich while the other guys started scouting the room. It was comforting that the man hadn't seen them and didn't know that they saw him. But there were lots of men in suits, and it wasn't easy to look at peoples' cheeks without attracting attention.

No one said much.

Eventually Willy returned with the ice cream sandwich and a knife. Ever tried to divide an ice cream sandwich in five pieces? As far as the boys were concerned, it was an operation as important and tricky as open-heart surgery.

They each enjoyed their single bite of treat, and Willy claimed the right to lick the wrapper.

Sam said, "You ice cream pig! We just had ice cream at the Freeze a few hours ago."

"That doesn't even seem like today," said Willy, looking shocked.

Jim interrupted. "He's not in here. Let's look somewhere else."

"Let's just start walking around. We're sure to spot him eventually," said Pete.

"Wait!"

"What, Jim? Do you see him?"

"That's him over there, in the middle of that circle of people." Jim paused for a second. "What are they doing?"

"I think they're reporters," said Pete. "Do you think they already found out what happened?"

"That's impossible," objected Chris. "The accident only happened an hour ago. And who would know about it other than us?"

"Maybe he confessed."

"The only way to find out is to go listen," Sam concluded.

They casually made their way over to the circle of people. What they heard surprised them. They arrived in time to hear the last part of one reporter's question, ". . . with the homeless. Do you feel we need new laws to cope with this problem, Senator Dunlap?"

"As you've heard me say many times before, we need to be fair. We need to be compassionate. We certainly can't ignore them. These people need our attention. We must have compassion and take whatever steps are necessary to help them get back on their feet."

86

The guys looked at each other in disbelief. A senator? Giving a speech about the homeless?

Another question came from the crowd, "Can you give us any specifics, Senator?"

The senator looked off into empty space for a moment before answering, "I'm afraid I can't give you the details at the moment, but I am working on some legislation that should significantly help those who find themselves in the homeless condition. My record is clear on this."

The Ringers couldn't believe what they were hearing.

CHOICE ⇒

If the guys quietly leave with their new information, turn to page 37.

If they decide to tell the reporters what they saw, turn to page 109.

Chris looked around at all the eyes staring at him. He decided he'd be a jerk to choose a squirt pen over the friendship of these guys.

"OK . . . I can get the pen another time." He was really bummed to have to pass up the fun he had waited so long for. But at the same time, he was relieved that he made the right choice.

"Good," said Pete, with a sense of finality, "then we're all set. Let's go for it."

Someone yelled, "Last one to the elevator has to smell Chris's shoes!" And the gang took off in an all-out sprint for the base of the monument.

Chris, being the fastest runner of the group (and also because he was probably the last person who wanted to smell his shoes!), was the first of the gang to reach the entrance. "Hey, guys! Where do we pay?" he yelled as the rest of the Ringers caught up to him.

"Excuse me, boys." The voice came from the lady in front of them. "You don't have to pay. It's free."

"All right! We can all go up *and* I can still get my squirt pen!"

Before long they were up in the point of the Washington Monument, peering down on a miniature-looking city.

"This is so great!" Jim was thrilled since he had never

seen a view like this in his life, except from airplanes. "You can see for miles!"

Sam got his camera out and looked through one of the small square windows. "Wow!" was all he could manage to say.

"What? What can you see?"

"Talk about seeing for miles! With this lens I can focus on buildings I can't even see just looking out the window. But even cooler is focusing on people and cars below. It's like they're in another world, and I'm looking in on them. I wonder if this is kind of how God sees us?"

"I think he sees us closer up than that." Pete was thinking out loud in response to Sam's question. "I mean, he doesn't need a telephoto lens to see us."

"But he does kinda look down on us, doesn't he?" Sam was carrying on the conversation but not turning his head from the view he was taking in.

"I guess. I don't know."

The concept was a little too heavy for everyone, and the conversation stalled.

Sam pulled the strap off his neck and handed the camera to Pete. "Here, everyone can have a look."

"Thanks, Sam," responded Pete. He put the camera to his eye and pointed it at the people below. "Man, they all look like ants."

"You should be able to see people better than that," Sam answered, slightly defensively.

"No, Sam, they look like ants. Wait! I know why. They *are* ants," Pete teased.

Everyone laughed, even Sam once he realized Pete was joking.

Turn to page 4.

This alarming piece of information threw everyone into a panic. John and Chip ran for the stairs, heading for the backyard and the freedom awaiting them on the other side of the fence.

Randy, now free from Chip's grip on his waist, started tilting like a seesaw. His feet lifted off the floor as his head slowly started leaning toward the ground outside.

He screamed. Not just a little yelp, but a full-fledged, blood curdling, horror movie scream.

Sam and Willy stood there with their mouths wide open but no sound coming out.

The police car came to a quick stop, and both officers jumped out to see what was going on. Seeing Randy hanging out his attic window with a camera in one hand made everything fairly clear.

What happened next will remain in Sam's and Willy's memory for the rest of their life.

The officers met them at the bottom of the attic stairs—right in Randy's upstairs hallway. "We have a pretty good idea what you boys were up to, but we'd sure like to hear it from your perspective."

John and Chip were gone, so Randy started right in with a lie. "We . . . uh . . . we were bird watching, yeah, that's what we were doing."

Both officers chuckled quietly.

Sam began to be sick to his stomach as he thought of the wrong they had been doing. He wanted to say something at many points along the way but couldn't muster the courage. But lying to the police on top of everything else was more than he could take. Now he couldn't take it any longer.

"That's a lie," he said with a strong voice.

Willy was thrilled that his friend obviously felt the same way he did. He could not understand how he had let things go so far without voicing his objection. It was a little late now, but he quickly decided it was time to stand with Sam. It was time to stand up for what he knew was right.

"Yeah, we weren't bird watching," Willy began slowly. "We were using this camera to spy on Ronda Turner—not that any of us even saw her."

One of the policemen affirmed, "That sounds more like the truth to me."

Randy was trying to save face. "Well, wait a minute. I wasn't lying. I said we were bird watching, and . . ." He paused to think through the rest of what he was going to say. It came out like this: "And Ronda's pretty like a bird. That's what I meant."

This time Sam and Willy were laughing with the officers.

The end result was awful. All three boys were taken down to the police station where their parents had to pick them up. Sam and Willy agreed later that they had come to a whole new understanding of the word *consequences*.

The good news was that Sam's and Willy's parents were glad they had told the truth to the police and didn't inflict huge punishments on them. They were both feeling pretty awful as it was.

The bad news was that Sam's parents decided he wasn't mature enough to own the camera. Even worse was telling his uncle Jeff why he couldn't keep it.

Life went on in Millersburg for Sam and Willy. But they learned that trying to sneak a look into someone's privacy doesn't just ruin your day; it can mess up your whole summer.

THE END

Turn to page 120.

Willy couldn't handle it. "Him?" he said real loud.

The man at the sink spun around to face the boys. They had caught him off guard. He smiled awkwardly and said, "Hello, boys. My name's Senator Dunlap. Were you looking for me?"

A senator? The guys looked at each other in astonishment, all thinking the same thing. *This is too much!*

Chris collected himself and played along. "Wow, Senator Dunlap, it really *is* you!"

Willy looked as terrified as he felt and, picking up on this, the senator looked straight at him and said, "Son, there's no reason to be nervous. I'm just a normal person like you."

Willy gulped. *This guy thinks I'm nervous because he's famous. Ha! If he only knew what we really know about him!*

The senator turned to Sam and said, "Did you want a picture to show at school, young man?"

"Huh?"

"I noticed you have a camera bag there. I assume you were looking for me in order to take your picture with me."

"Yes sir!" Chris jumped into the conversation again. "That's exactly what we want—your picture."

"Well, you boys gather around me, and you'll get just what you want."

Holding back a huge grin that wanted to appear on his face, Pete said, "God sure worked this out for us, huh, guys?"

The senator chuckled. "A man of faith, eh? I like that. Where would this country be without boys like you? I bet you don't even know what drugs look like."

Sam focused the camera and took two pictures—just to make sure they got a good one.

Chris was getting more confident about their secret. "Senator Dunlap, that's a bad-looking cut. What did you do to your cheek?"

The senator suddenly got cold toward the gang. They noticed his attitude change immediately. The senator fumbled for words for a few seconds before answering, distantly, "Well, even senators can be a little absentminded sometimes. Would you believe I tripped over a garbage can?"

"Of course we'd believe that. Shoot, we might have even guessed it." Chris smiled at his friends.

They didn't smile back. He could see by their expressions that they thought he was pushing his luck.

"Senator Dunlap?" Chris asked just as the senator was headed for the bathroom door. "Can I ask one more question?"

"Of course, young man."

Chris hated being called "young man." As sarcastic as he was, he wanted to return the favor by calling the senator "middle-aged man." He bit his tongue and refrained. "I'd be interested in knowing what you think kids like us can do to serve our country."

Senator Dunlap smiled and turned toward the boys. "Just love your fellowman," he said smoothly. "And keep believing in God," he added, looking straight at Pete.

"You mean just be nice to people and try to help them?" Jim responded in obvious astonishment.

"Suuuure. You know—get involved in your community, volunteer at a—" He took a deep breath. ". . . homeless shelter, stuff like that."

No one knew how to respond. Jim muttered, "Uh . . . uh . . ." fishing for words.

Finally, Chris said, "Thanks for your time."

The senator smiled and walked out the door.

CHOICE ⇒

If the gang talks about their findings right there in the rest room, turn to page 8.

If they quietly leave the building and talk outside, turn to page 22.

"**C**ome on, guys, knock it off! We're gonna miss her," Chip said, not caring about the condition of the window or the camera.

"Forget it!" Sam shouted. He grabbed his camera from Chip and inspected it for damage.

John decided to try to settle things down. "Chill out, guys! Give Chip the camera before Ronda gets into the shower."

"Don't do it, Sam. This whole thing was wrong from the start." Willy couldn't believe he was saying this. "Maybe this is God's way of stopping us from doing something that we'll regret."

"I don't care about God. I gotta figure out how to fix this window. Everyone out!" Randy yelled. He looked at Sam and Willy and said, "Don't you twirps ever bring that thing around here again. You guys got me in big trouble!"

Sam was about to remind Randy about whose idea this was, but Willy pulled him toward the door before Sam could open his mouth.

Once they were outside, Sam decided that they should go to the Freeze and talk about what they should really do with the camera.

CHOICE ⇒

Turn to page 68.

Silence settled on the gang like a wet blanket. Sam had his head between his legs, hoping that more blood to his brain would help him come up with the answer. Jim and Chris shuffled their feet and stared at the ground. Pete stood tall and proud, waiting to squash any incorrect guesses.

Willy broke the silence. "Dude!"

Startled, everyone riveted their eyes on Willy, waiting to hear his theory.

"It's like this: you all know Mark Newhouse, right?" Mark was a really popular kid at their school.

"I don't know him." Jim had only lived in the United States for about a month and didn't know anyone from the school yet.

Willy turned his attention toward Jim. "Mark's this guy from school who can do anything and do it well. He gets fantastic grades in all his classes, and all the girls think he's a stud." He turned to the other boys as he continued. "And as I'm sure all of you remember, he's the point guard on the basketball team as well as the student government president."

With this last statement he stopped, holding his hands out expectantly. But no one responded.

"Don't you get it?" Willy was gaining confidence in his answer and launched into a full explanation: "Newhouse is *point* guard and *president!* Pete said the view from the point was great, but the president had never seen it. It all fits."

That sounds like a reasonable answer, all the remaining boys thought. They looked expectantly to Pete for some sign that Willy was correct.

"What a joke!" Pete said, laughing. "That's the most ridiculous answer I've ever heard!"

Willy's face dropped. He thought he had finally solved one of Pete's stupid riddles. "What's so dumb about it?" he asked.

"You didn't solve the riddle," Pete said, getting more serious. "You made a stab at figuring out what *point* and *president* meant. But you didn't think about an answer. Are we supposed to go look for an adventure at Mark Newhouse's? Get real!"

CHOICE ⇒

Well, this answer sure wasn't right. Go back to page 68 and try a different answer to Pete's riddle.

The scene would have erupted into complete chaos if John hadn't stepped in and said, "Chill out, guys. Your camera's fine, weasel." Sam scowled at him. "And Randy, we'll just put a rock up here and your parents will think someone tossed it through the window—problem solved."

Willy thought to himself that Randy's parents might wonder why all the broken glass was down on the lawn rather than up in the attic, but he decided not to say anything.

Everyone's attention was quickly drawn back to the window when Randy whispered very loudly, "There's Ronda!" He grabbed the camera from Chip, who was pretty glad to get rid of it after the window incident.

All five boys crammed around the tiny window. "Stop pushing!" said Randy with an irritated voice. They all leaned back about an inch. No one wanted to step too far back and miss the action.

Randy continued speaking as he tried to get a good glimpse of Ronda. "Oh, man, I can't get a good angle from here. That tree's right in the middle. If I can just stick my head out the window I should have a straight shot."

"Well hurry up 'cause your time's almost up," John said impatiently.

Randy opened the latch on the window and swung it open. "Hold on to my waist so I don't fall if I lean too far."

Randy was skinny enough that he could fit his head and shoulders through the window frame.

The next two sentences out of Randy's mouth made the boys' stomachs go up and down like the biggest drop on the biggest roller coaster in the world.

First he said, "This is great, I can see perfectly from here."

But it was quickly followed by, "Cops!" A patrol car was slowly driving down their street.

CHOICE ⟹

If some of the boys panic and take off running, turn to page 90.

If all five boys stay put and stay quiet, turn to page 79.

When Chris returned to the group, it quickly became obvious that Chris's punishment for being selfish about the money had already begun—cold shoulders from the guys. He regretted his decision but had too much pride to admit it and offer the money to Jim right then.

"Then the Capitol building it is," Pete summed up the conversation that had taken place while Chris was walking back. "It's free, so we can use our money on other things."

"Yeah, like electro-laser-phaser pens!" Sam joked.

Everyone had a good laugh except Chris.

It was a beautiful day, and the guys enjoyed their walk along the park called the Mall.

By the time they got to the Capitol, everyone was pretty tired. But Jim wouldn't let them rest for a second. He had never been to any of these places. "What do you think you're doing, sitting down?" He couldn't believe they would stop that close to going inside.

Jim won. The gang all trudged up the stairs and inside the rotunda.

After looking around for a while, they got bored and went back outside. Then Pete got an idea. "Look guys, this isn't the Washington Monument, but there's still a pretty good view of the Mall from here."

"What mall? I don't see any stores," joked Sam.

"Ha, ha, ha," Pete answered with no emotion at all.

"The whole reason we came to the city was to try Sam's camera and lens. And the view from here is better than anything else we'll find around home."

Willy joined the conversation. "Yeah, let's do it. There're tons of people in the Mall. Let's check 'em out."

Sam didn't need much convincing; he had started to wonder if they'd forgotten about his cool gift. He pulled it out of its bag and put the lens on before anyone had a chance to disagree.

It was only fair for him to look first since it was his camera. All the other boys plopped down while Sam started scanning the Mall. He had a humongous smile on his face.

"What are you grinning about?" asked Willy. "You look like you're making a goofy face and someone's about to take a picture of you!"

Sam answered without lowered the camera from his face. "This is just so cool! I can see *everything*. It's like watching TV with the sound turned down—I can see people's lips moving, but I can't hear anything."

"We'll add the sound for you," joked Willy. "Oh, Penelope," he started with a quivering voice, "your eyes are like limping pools."

"That's limpid pools, you dufas," corrected Pete.

Willy elbowed Jim to respond.

Without a second's break, Jim continued the make-believe conversation. "Oh, Walter," Jim was talking in a high girlish voice, "you're such a stud-man!"

Willy and Jim faked a big kissing sound and erupted

104

into laughter, lightly punching each other so no one would think they weren't acting.

"You guys, that didn't fit what I'm watching," Sam interrupted in a serious tone. Everyone got quiet.

"There's a man and a woman talking, all right," Sam explained. "But it's not very friendly."

"Can I look?" a voice asked.

The question was very quiet, almost unnoticeable. Sam turned around to see Chris. He hadn't spoken one word since the squirt pen conversation. The funny thing was, he hadn't even bought the pen. Now, with everyone looking at him, he just sat there waiting for an answer from Sam.

CHOICE ⇉

Sam has a tough choice to make. The action Sam is watching is about to get terribly interesting. He doesn't want to miss it, but Chris asked. If Sam hands the camera over to Chris, turn to page 115.

If Sam asks Chris to wait a minute more, turn to page 31.

Pete was a logical thinker, even when he was afraid. "Guys, we're in way over our heads here. Let's just give the film to Mr. Rey and go home. Besides, who'd believe a bunch of kids like us anyway—except *maybe* my dad?"

Everyone but Chris picked up on the clue. Sam even started winding the film so he could take it out of the camera.

Chris was frustrated. He didn't understand why they were all going along with Pete's plan. But he was scared too and didn't really want to add to their problem. So he just stood there huffing and looking around frantically.

In fact, Chris was huffing and puffing so much he was almost hyperventilating. Had it not been such a tense moment, someone probably would have teased him about sounding like the big bad wolf.

While everyone, including Mr. Rey, was looking at Chris, Sam got gutsy and popped the film out of the camera into his camera bag. He quickly reached into the bag and pulled out a different roll of used film, which he had shot on the subway as they were traveling into D.C.

"Here . . . here's the film." Sam held out the roll toward the man.

"But . . . but . . . ," Chris sputtered. He couldn't believe their big chance at exposing a serious crime was ending like a bad dream.

"You boys did the right thing," said Mr. Rey. "Senator

Dunlap is a good man and a great politician. There's no need to let a little mishap like this ruin his career." With the Ringers' subway ride in his suit pocket, Mr. Rey left the rest room.

No one said a word—except Chris. He just kept repeating, "I can't believe it. . . . I can't believe it. . . ."

Once the gang was back outside, and a few blocks from the library, Sam spoke up. He wanted to make sure they were a safe distance from Mr. Rey.

"Guys, stop, I have something to show you." With that he pulled the roll of film from his camera bag.

Chris said, "So what? A roll of film. What good will that do us now that you gave the real stuff to—" Chris stopped. The reality of what had happened hit him all at once. "You switched rolls?"

Sam smiled and bowed. "Yes, master."

Willy laughed and said, "Sammy, you stud-man! You *total, complete* stud-man! That was smoothness to the max!"

"Thank you. Thank you," Sam kept saying.

Congratulations and compliments showered Sam for the rest of the day. And when the real film got into the hands of Pete's dad, the gang decided they'd handled the situation better than any TV cop they'd ever seen.

Chris even said, "Someone should write a book about this!"

"Or make a movie!" added Willy. "Hey, maybe we should . . ."

THE END

Turn to page 120.

"I hate this." Willy sat on the bench trying to come up with an answer, but he couldn't. And he didn't really hate Pete's riddles. They were fun if—but only if—you didn't guess wrong.

Pete started tapping his foot on the ground. He was trying to bug everyone. It was working. He tapped it faster.

"Cut that out before I chop your toes off!" Chris said. Willy and Sam shouted in agreement, and all three boys lost interest in their answer quest momentarily.

Jim interrupted the babble with a quiet word that somehow caught everyone's attention. "Washington."

"What did you say?" Pete inquired.

"You said 'D.C.' before you started the riddle." Jim calmly started explaining his reasoning. "So it's got to be somewhere in the city."

Sam objected, "But you just moved here. You don't know anything about Washington, D.C."

"Sure I do," Jim reacted. "We studied all about it in my schoolwork in Brazil."

Pete was impatient. "Fine, fine, let's hear your answer."

Jim continued, "Well, here it is: The Washington Monument is a tall column with a point on top, right?"

Sam didn't get it. "Yeah, so what. Pete's head has a

point on top also!" Willy joined Sam in an eruption of laughter.

Jim ignored them and finished his conclusions. "The Washington Monument was built years after George Washington died, so he never saw the view from the point. And it would be a great place to try the camera and lens."

Pete smiled. "Bingo! That's the answer."

Sam jumped in with, "Oh, man, I can't believe the guy from the jungles of Brazil figured out something in our own backyard!"

"Good job, Jim." Willy congratulated his friend. Then he added, "And that's a fantastic idea, Pete." All the other boys agreed.

Chris got all excited and sealed the conversation with, "My mom is taking Jill and Tina into the city to go shopping. So we could ride the train with them, and we wouldn't need a chaperone." Jill, Chris's cousin, was visiting for the summer. Tina was Jim's sister.

Sam stood up from the bench, put his camera bag over his shoulder, and said, "It's my camera, and I say let's do it! Everyone go home and get permission. We'll meet at the train station at noon."

With that, all five boys headed in separate directions, eager to start their adventure.

CHOICE

Turn to page 59.

"**H**ow can you say that?" blurted out Jim.

All the reporters looked at him, and the guys in the gang stared at him. Its a good thing eyebrows don't make noise when they go up, or else there would have been a real roar in the cafeteria.

Senator Dunlap just smiled and said, "Do you have a problem with helping the homeless, son?"

Jim scowled. "No, I have a problem with you saying you care about the homeless when you just hit one with your car in an alley a few blocks from here and left without reporting the accident. For all you know, that lady could be dead right now."

A gasp ran through the crowd. Reporters started writing like crazy in their little notepads. Chris, Pete, Willy, and Sam stared at Jim with their mouths hanging open.

Jim turned to his friends and quietly said, "Sorry, guys. I just couldn't listen to his lies." No one responded.

The senator just laughed.

That made Jim even angrier. "You can go ahead and laugh. I've got proof!"

"What proof?" the senator asked with a serious face and a threatening tone. Some of the reporters mumbled back and forth anxiously.

Sam answered for Jim—he knew there was no turning back on what Jim had started, and he figured he might as well jump in. "We've got photos right here." He tapped his camera.

"Pictures of the accident?" asked another reporter.

The senator started to shake and sweat. He loosened his tie and opened his top shirt button.

"No," Sam responded. He pointed to Jim. "He saw the accident. We've got pictures of his car."

"Pictures of my car?" Senator Dunlap said with a little relieved smile. The mood was incredibly tense. Reporters wheeled around to look at the senator. "Anyone could take pictures of my car!"

"Yeah, but our pictures show the dent in your hood where you hit the lady. We've also got a picture of a bloody handkerchief you left on your dashboard."

The circle of reporters wheeled around again. Their presence made the guys more comfortable with this than they expected. Chris, in his normally abrasive manner, started in next. "Why don't you tell us, Mr. Senator, how you got that terrible scrape on your cheek?"

The reporters turned their attention back to the senator. A few of them continued to scribble notes on their pads without looking down at what they were writing.

Senator Dunlap paused for an uncomfortably long time. Sweat ran down from his forehead, stinging the fresh, red abrasion that everyone was staring at.

"I told you," he said, looking at the reporters. "I . . . uh . . . tripped over my son's bike in the driveway this morning."

One of the reporter's laughed. "Uh, you've got a little problem here, Senator. You flew into town this morning from New York. You were never at your home here in Washington."

None of the boys had ever seen someone have a nervous breakdown, but they had a vague idea of what it must be. And it looked like that was what Senator Dunlap was having.

His shaking got worse. He started mumbling incoherently and fumbling with his hands.

By the time he'd been taken away by police, the reporters had taken statements from all the guys. And new pictures were taken—this time of the Ringers.

The guys never had to prove anything. The senator later confessed to the hit-and-run accident.

On their way out of the Health building an hour later, Pete asked the rest of the guys, "Did we do the right thing? I mean, we just ended the career of a well-known politician."

Jim corrected their thoughts. "*We* didn't end his career. *He* did."

They headed for the place they were to meet Chris's mom.

THE END
Turn to page 120.

After finding the man's car and taking several pictures of it, the gang proceeded into the government building.

They stood in the main lobby looking at a map of the building.

"This place is huge! How do we know where to look?" asked Jim.

"Yeah," Willy agreed, "we could spend three days in here and not cover everything."

"I've got an idea," offered Pete.

"Of course you do," said Chris. "What do you want us to do—ask the lady at the information desk where the man in the suit is?"

Willy and Sam started snickering. But as usual, Pete ignored them and went on explaining his idea. "We need to split up."

Chris continued teasing. He started shaking and whining. "Help me, help me! I'm splitting up!"

"Well, you're definitely cracked!" said Jim.

"If we each take a floor," Pete reasoned, "and agree to look quickly, then return in twenty minutes, we might find him real fast."

Pete's ideas usually didn't have flaws. This one did. Jim saw it first. "Pete, there's a little problem with your idea."

Chris put a fake expression of shock on his face.

"What? The rocket scientist has a flawed plan? In-con-*ceivable!*"

This time it was Jim's turn to ignore Chris. As usual, Willy and Sam were in hysterics.

Jim reasoned, "The problem with splitting up is that no one's seen the guy but me."

Pete smacked himself on the head. "Of course! What an idiot!"

"No argument there," mumbled Sam.

"Yeah," Chris added, "we've always thought you were an idiot."

Jim looked Chris right in the eye and said, "Chris, sometimes you take things too far! Do you ever say anything nice to Pete?"

Chris was caught off guard. He didn't have an answer and just looked down.

After a few seconds of thinking, Chris sucked in his pride and said, "Sorry, Pete. You do have pretty good ideas—*most* of the time."

Jim shook his head and sighed.

"Hey, look," Chris defended himself, "it's not easy being less smart than Pete!"

"Thanks," Pete said, smiling.

"Just chill out, Chris," said Sam. "Let Pete do what he's good at, and you do what you're good at. We freak people out when we put ourselves together like that."

Chris laughed. "Good point."

Willy broke up the solemn moment. "Like the many parts of the body," he said, holding his hand to his chest

114

and staring into space, "so is our gang of Ringers—one, yet many. Many, yet one."

He broke into laughter, as did the rest of them.

"OK, here's the plan," offered Sam. "Only Jim actually saw the man. But we do know one thing: he's probably got a scuffed cheek."

"Yeah, it looked like he cut it pretty bad," agreed Jim.

"So let's walk around the main areas first. Jim can look for him, but we should all keep our eyes open for any men in suits who have a scuffed cheek."

"That still doesn't tell us where to look," Willy said quietly.

"Well, I'd say we either start with the main hallway or the cafeteria," Pete suggested.

Chris agreed.

CHOICE ⇔

If the gang starts looking in the main hallway, turn to page 56.

If they go to the cafeteria, turn to page 84.

Sam hesitated. *Chris was such a jerk earlier. But he is a good friend and a pretty reliable guy.*

"OK." Sam took the strap off his neck and carefully handed the camera over to Chris.

"Thanks," said Chris with more warmth in his voice than any of the guys had expected.

"No problem, buddy." Everyone was relieved that the tension with Chris was finally over. Things could now return to normal.

Chris hoisted the equipment up and pressed the back of the camera against his face, peering across the reflecting pool over to the park.

The mood changed abruptly.

"Oh, man!" Chris gasped.

"What?"

"What's goin' on?"

"What do you see?"

It was a chorus of questions from the gang. They were dying to know what caused Chris's gasp.

"She must be a thief!"

"Who? Who must be a thief?"

"The lady. You know, the lady you saw arguing with the man." Chris went on to explain what he saw. "She kicked him, and he's down on the ground. And she's stealing stuff from his coat pocket. Now she's running away. Oh, man, he's so-o-o mad! He's screaming at her—wait! He's starting to run after her!"

Each guy was visualizing the action in his own mind, causing his heart to beat faster and faster with excitement.

Chris continued after a short pause, "No! He's down on the ground again. He must be in too much pain."

Pete, the always-thinking member of the Ringers, interrupted. "Guys!" There was a sense of urgency in his voice. "What should we do about this? Don't you think we should do something? I mean, we can't just watch, right?"

No one said anything. They were all staring blankly at Pete as they had earlier when he posed the riddle. It took a few moments for the surprise of Pete's questions to wear off.

CHOICE ⇔

If the Ringers decide the best response is to do nothing, turn to page 64.

If the gang decides to tell a nearby policeman what they've seen, turn to page 24.

If they run over to help the man, turn to page 46.

It wasn't easy for the guys to find the alley where the lady got hit. Things look a lot different on the ground than they do from the sky.

"There it is," announced Jim with relief.

Willy, getting more nervous with every step, questioned, "How can you be sure that's the right alley?"

"Duh!" Chris shot back. "Don't you think the ambulance and cop cars are a good clue?"

The security guard in the monument had reached people to help.

Willy continued: "We should probably be pretty quiet about what we saw, since we don't know what the truth really is."

"Yeah, I agree," affirmed Sam. "Let's just listen and see what information we can pick up."

Their plan worked. As the paramedics lifted the old lady onto a stretcher, one of them said, "I still don't understand how a guard in the Washington Monument had the information to call us about this accident."

It seemed their call was the only report. The paramedics didn't mention someone calling from the Health building.

Then a policeman made a comment that caught each boy's attention. He said to his partner, "Well, if she dies it's just one less street bum this city has to worry about."

The guys were shocked. How could anyone care so little about another person's life?

Jim didn't understand. "I don't get it. What did he mean by 'a street bum'?"

Pete was visibly angry. "He's talking about a homeless person. What a jerk. You'd think someone who works on the streets would have more compassion for the problems of homeless people."

"Why are they homeless? You mean they're just too lazy to get a job?"

"I keep forgetting that you haven't lived here in the States before this summer. And you've got it all wrong— but then so do lots of people who've lived here all their lives."

Chris took over the explanation. "Yeah, so many Americans think that homeless people are lazy bums. I guess I used to think so, too. But we talked about them once with our old Sunday school teacher, Miss Whitehead—"

"You mean my grandpa's sister."

"Oh, yeah, I forgot. Anyhow, most homeless people aren't lazy at all. They've just had some lousy things happen to them and find themselves with no way to make any money—not even enough for food."

Pete finished off the thought. "And without a place to live or any money at all, they end up in the streets of big cities, hoping for food and a break in life."

"So the lady I saw get hit was one of those?"

"It sounds like it from what that cop said."

By this time the ambulance was gone, and one of the

officers turned to the boys and said, "Nothing to see here, boys. Move along."

The guys were stunned as they walked away. They had witnessed a major crime—the hit-and-run of a homeless lady in an alley—a lady who might even die with no one to care about it.

After walking in silence for a block, heading nowhere in particular, Jim quietly asked, "Do you think we should go to the Health building and see if we can take the guy's picture?"

Everyone stopped.

Chris's eyes lit up as he answered, "Yeah! Jim knows what he looks like, and it won't even be dangerous because we don't need to get very close to him."

CHOICE ⇒

If the gang heads over to the library to look for the man, turn to page 33.

If they decide not to get involved because it might be dangerous, turn to page 81.

120

Sam's camera gave the Ringers a bit more than they expected. If you're curious about what else might have happened, don't be shy—start again and make other choices. Who knows what the gang will find?

Make sure you haven't missed any of the other Ringers' Choice Adventures. This ever-expanding gang of energetic explorers just can't seem to have a normal day! Get to know Sam, Willy, Pete, Chris, Jim, Jill, Tina, and others. You may even want to become a Ringer yourself.

Mark Oestreicher is a pastor to junior highers and former editor of *Teen Power*, a Sunday school take-home paper for eleven-to-fourteen-year-olds. He lives with his wife, Jeannie, in Omaha, Nebraska.